THE SONG OF A SCARECROW

Written and illustrated by

SUDDHASATTWA BASU

KATHA

"I am sick and tired of standing in one place. I want to be free," the scarecrow said to himself.

Next day at the crack of dawn, the scarecrow left the little patch of cornfield that he had been guarding for ages.

On his way he met a cow.
"Good Morning, Cow," he said,
"Coming for a stroll with me?"

"Wish I could," the cow said, "But my child needs to be fed and my master will be coming for milk. Sorry Scarecrow, I have work to do."

Bidding goodbye to the cow, the scarecrow came to the riverside. He stepped on to a little boat and drifted aimlessly.

"Hop into my boat," he said to the little fish swimming in the water.

“I will die if I jump out from the water,” said the little fish and disappeared into the depth of the river, leaving a ripple of delicate bubbles behind.

The scarecrow enjoyed his
new found freedom ... chasing
butterflies busy collecting nectar,

... mimicking birds building nests,

... and running across the meadow,
following the shadows of
waterbearing clouds.

"This is life," he cried with joy, "I am free and I am happy." He stuck a bunch of wild flowers in his hat and then, buzzed off after a swarm of busy bees.

By noon our scarecrow felt a little tired. He sat down under the cool shade of an old banyan tree and dozed off to sleep.

When he woke up, the sun was about to set, turning everything around him into gold with its midas touch. It was the same glorious sunset that the scarecrow had seen many times from his little cornfield.

He felt homesick. He stood up slowly ...
and with a heart that grew happier by the
minute, started homewards.

When he reached home, the scarecrow couldn't believe his eyes. The piece of land, which, until this morning was full of healthy corn, looked like a devastated battlefield!

Every corn was eaten!
Every leaf was torn!
Every plant pulled out from its roots!

The scarecrow felt very, very sad.
Something churned inside his
stomach and a lump stuck in
his throat.

His eyes became moist. A tear rolled down his round cheek and settled on a dry leaf like a gleaming dew drop.

"I was happy. And now I am sad," the scarecrow could hardly utter these words in his choked voice.

Since then the earth has taken another round of the sun. And time has left no scars on the face of the earth. Healthy corn once again sway gently in the southern breeze and amidst the undulating green sea of corn, our scarecrow stands tall and happy. Forever.

At night when the rising mist spreads a smoky veil across the field, the scarecrow looks up at the starry sky and sings his song, a lullaby for the baby corn.

"On a cold night when the stars shine
And the southern breeze ruffles your hair,
I find my world in you, babies
I'm happy because you are mine.

“When it drizzles or it pours
Pearly drops in monsoon times,
I find my ocean in you, babies
I’m happy because you are mine.

"When the sky's painted in rainbow lines
And the silence whispers all around,
I find my freedom in you, babies
I'm happy because you are mine.

“When you leave in autumn days
The distant bells faintly chime,
I’m happy to see you going, babies
And wait for others to become mine.”

The baby corn fall asleep listening to his song, waking up the next day, slightly bigger.

Suddhasattwa Basu is a renowned illustrator, painter and animation filmmaker. This is his first book for children as a writer.

KATHA

Printed at RaveIndia, New Delhi

KATHA is a registered nonprofit devoted to enhancing the joys of reading amongst children and adults. Katha Schools are situated in the slums and streets of Delhi and tribal villages of Arunachal Pradesh.
A3 Sarvodaya Enclave, Sri Aurobindo Marg
New Delhi 110 017
Phone: 4141 6600 . 4182 9998 . 2652 1752
Fax: 2651 4373
E-mail: marketing@katha.org, Website: www.katha.org

Ten per cent of sales proceeds from this book will support the quality education of children studying in Katha Schools.
Katha regularly plants trees to replace the wood used in the making of its books.

First Reprint 2004, Second Reprint 2012